Densey Clyne's Small

It's a Frog's Life!

A
LITTLE
ARK
BOOK

ALLEN & UNWIN

The life cycle of a frog

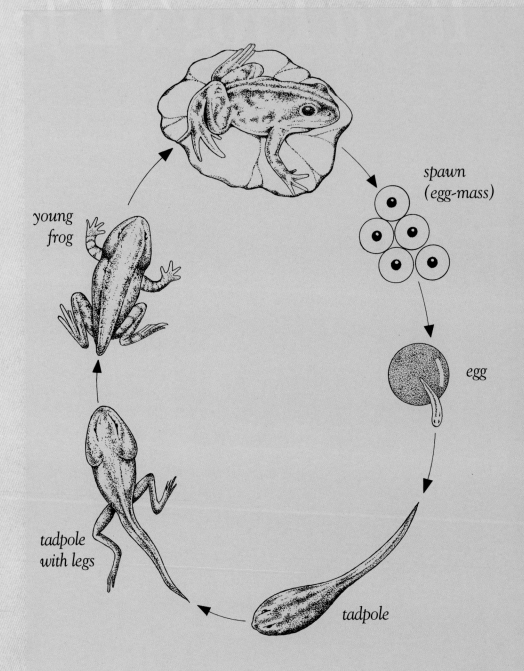

spawn
(egg-mass)

young
frog

egg

tadpole
with legs

tadpole

What and why, how and where

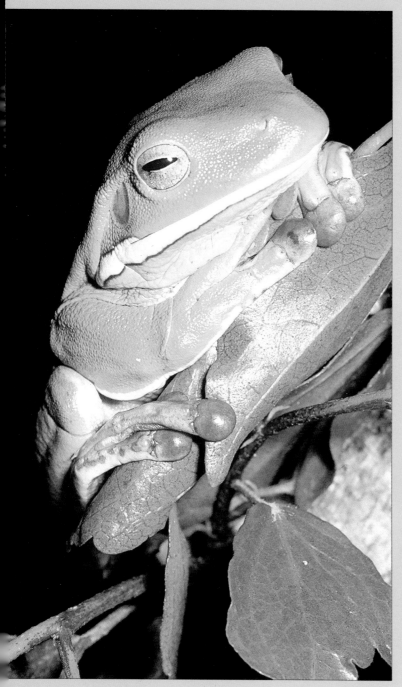

Giant tree frog

What's the first thing you notice when you look at a frog? Perhaps it's those bulging eyes, or the long legs folded so neatly, or the wide mouth. And why do some frogs seem to wear a big smile all the time? Surely life's not *that* easy for a frog!

Well, big eyes and long legs and a wide mouth are very important to a frog's way of life. In this book you'll find out why. You'll see how frogs spend their time up in the trees, down on the ground, and in the water.

You'll see where frogs live, how they catch their food and avoid their enemies. You'll find out why some frogs can leap and climb while others are earthbound. What frogs must do to survive in the desert. Why they have such loud voices. When they meet to mate.

And you'll discover how you can become a frog-watcher.

First, find your frog

If you haven't done much frog-watching, you may think it's easy to find a frog. It's not! If frogs were easy to find, their predators, such as snakes and birds, would eat them all up.

Frogs like to live in watery places with somewhere to hide. The pond in the picture has lots of vegetation in the water and around the edges. It could make a safe home for three or four different kinds of frog. For some little frogs, even a rain puddle can make a temporary home.

The perfect home for a frog—a pond with vegetation

Northern banjo frog hiding in its watery home

Frog-hunting is best done on summer nights when a frog chorus can lead you to their hiding place. One thing is certain: by the time you get there, all the frogs will have stopped singing.

Frogs are good ventriloquists. When you try to track one down by its call, it will *always* turn out to be further away than you think—usually on the other side of the pond or creek! With luck your torch may pick out one that's floating nearby. If you're quiet and patient the chorus may start up again.

Come sing along with me

You can tell a male frog by the 'bubble' under his chin. Nearly all male frogs have this inflatable sac (called a vocal sac) in their throat. They fill it with air to make their calls louder. Only male frogs make calls and join choruses. They call to attract female frogs to the water when they are ready to breed.

The Brown-striped frog in the picture was interrupted in the middle of his call so his vocal sac is partly deflated. He's the frog that makes the loud 'tok! tok! tok!' sound like a wood-chopper at work.

Brown-striped frog

Mosquitoes on the head of a tropical Wood frog

The tropical Wood frogs from far north Queensland have two vocal sacs. Once when I camped by a rainforest river I could hear their unusual calls loud and clear above the rain and the rushing river. Frogs in noisy places need loud voices.

When male frogs of the same kind call in chorus, some calls are high-pitched, some are low. It depends on the size of the frog. Each male frog takes it in turn to call. This way, they avoid confusing the females they're trying to attract.

See the mosquitoes on the frog's head in the picture? These mosquitoes love frog's blood—in fact they drink nothing else!

Red-eyed tree frog

Each male frog has a signature 'tune' that identifies his *species* (a group of animals or plants with the same habits and appearance). His call sends two messages. To other males it says: 'This is my territory, keep out or else!' To females it says: 'Come on over, let's make tadpoles together!'

Most frogs need water to breed in, but they don't only call from the water. You'll often find a tree frog calling from shrubs and bushes or high up in a tree. Some frogs call from under the eaves of houses.

Frogs keep their cool

Slender tree frog cooling off in a flower

Well-watered gardens are often home to one or two kinds of frog. A garden can make a very suitable habitat, especially in warm climates where plants grow lush and provide daytime shelter all year round.

Leaves stay cool in hot weather by evaporating moisture, so a garden plant is a good hiding place for frogs on a hot day. You may come across a frog asleep in the greenhouse, hidden in a hanging basket on the verandah or even sitting in a garden flower.

A full watering can (left) or a dripping tap (below) can make a good home for a frog

Frogs are good at finding cracks and crevices that are permanently damp. But as hiding places these can turn out to be not so permanent!

A little frog once lived in my watering can. I kept the water topped up and took photographs of the frog peering out at me. Imagine if it had chosen the nozzle of my hose instead—it would have been jetted out at high speed!

Frogs must stay damp and cool to survive. They can soak up water through their skin, but they also *dehydrate*, or lose water, the same way. Once they dehydrate they can die very quickly.

A good place for a frog in the tropical north of Australia and in the dry outback is an outside water tank with a dripping tap.

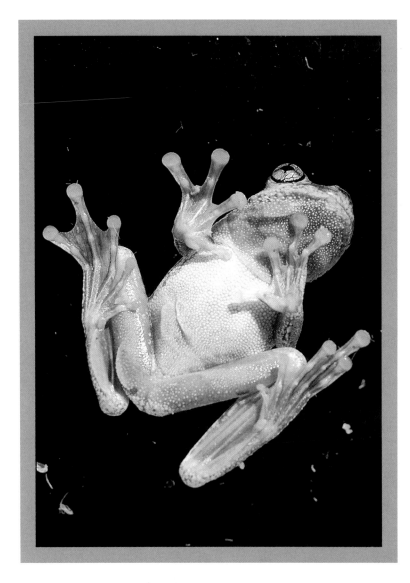

Peron's tree frog waiting for insects on a lit window

A likely place to find a frog on a summer night is near a lit window. It may seem to be peering in but it's not really people-watching. For frogs, a lit window is like a free snack bar because moths and other insects are drawn there by the light.

This gives us a chance to look at the underside of the frog. The disc-like toes and fingers tell us it's a tree frog. Only a tree frog can climb vertical surfaces such as walls and windows.

We call a frog's front limbs its 'arms', and talk about its hands and fingers. Frogs are among the very few animals that share those names with us.

Looking, leaping, listening

A tree frog usually goes hunting among the leaves for insects, and catches them by leaping. Its big, wide-apart eyes help it judge the distance from its prey; broad fingers and toes help it land safely on target; and the wide mouth makes sure of a catch.

You might wonder how frogs can see in the dark. But nights are never really pitch black, as we find out for ourselves when we give our eyes time to adjust.

Slender tree frog

Green and golden bell frog

Tree frogs don't all live in trees. Notice the small toes and fingers on this Green and golden bell frog. It spends a lot of time in the water, often calling by day. The call sounds nothing like a bell—more a 'crawwwwk! crok-crok!' sound.

It's important for frogs to hear each other's calls. If you look at the picture you can see what a frog's ear looks like; it's the round patch behind its eye. Our eardrums are hidden away inside our sticking-out ear flaps. A frog has its eardrums on the outside, and no ear flaps.

The proper name for a frog's ear is *tympanum*, which is another word for drum. On some frogs the tympanum is quite hard to see.

Know your enemies

Crested hawk feeding a tree frog to her chicks

A frog's sharp hearing, big eyes and long legs can usually help it escape from enemies—but not always.

Birds and snakes are the frog's worst enemies. Birds hunt by sight, snakes hunt by smell, and some only feed on frogs.

Crested hawks feed mainly on tree frogs and stick insects. This female has brought a tropical tree frog for her chicks to squabble over. Tree frogs are a favourite of these yellow-eyed raptors. Hungry nestlings like these can drastically reduce the frog population.

Slender tree frog well-camouflaged on a leaf

A frog's best defence against birds is camouflage.

By day this tree frog rests on a leaf with arms and legs neatly folded, to disguise its shape and hide its bright colours.

But bright colours can also help a frog escape.

'Flash' colours hidden in the groins and armpits of some frogs can help them escape when their camouflage fails. The frog leaps away, suddenly exposing patches of colour that just as suddenly disappear when it moves. This confuses the enemy long enough for the frog to make its getaway.

'Flash' colours on Peron's tree frog

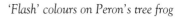

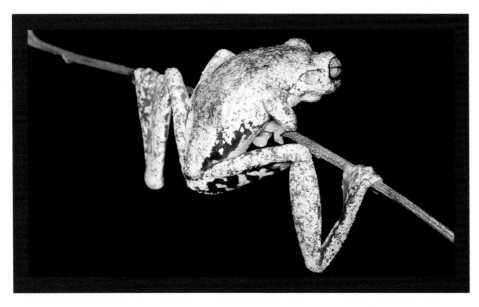

Egret looking for frogs

Frogs that live mainly on the ground and in the water have the same enemies: snakes and birds. Wading birds such as herons and egrets feed mainly on frogs. These birds are very clever at finding frogs hidden in the reeds and water.

    In these situations the same rules apply—try not to look like a frog, find a good hiding place and don't move! If this doesn't work *bluff it out* like the frog on page 17.

A frog can inflate itself to look too big to eat

This frog's not really fat: it has simply inflated its lungs to make itself look too big to swallow. This is a defence often used when a frog finds itself caught in the open by a bird or a snake. Perhaps this frog thought my camera was a frog-eater!

Rainforest frogs have many hiding places. Underneath the dense cover of fallen leaves it's damp and cool, but even in the open a small frog seems to disappear from sight.

A rainforest frog well-camouflaged on a fallen leaf

Table manners

The places frogs like to live in are also popular with insects. Bees and wasps drink there. Bugs skate above, diving beetles swim below. Dragonflies lay their eggs and their nymphs develop in the water.

For several hours this newly emerged dragonfly will be at risk from hungry frogs. If it moved it could be down a frog's throat before you could say 'tok'.

The insect would be helped on its way, believe it or not, by the frog's bulging eyes. When a frog swallows, its eyeballs sink inwards and press down against its tongue to push the food down. That's why a frog screws up its face and blinks every time it swallows!

A young dragonfly is prey for a hungry frog

Peron's tree frog watching for insects

Crucifix frog picking up an ant with its tongue

Unlike ours, a frog's tongue is fixed at the front of its mouth. Frogs actually catch their food by flicking their tongues in and out quickly.

This Crucifix frog gets its name from the cross-like pattern on its back. Crucifix frogs feed on termites and ants. Not many animals will touch ants, but this frog will sit by an ant trail for hours and pick off the ants one by one.

A specialist

The brightly patterned Corroboree frog

The Corroboree frog is one of our prettiest little animals and looks more like an enamelled brooch than a frog. Its name comes from the colour pattern, which resembles Aboriginal art.

The reason for such vivid colouring is a mystery because this tiny frog lives hidden away in dense, cushiony mats of sphagnum moss where few predators would see it.

There's even a striking contrast of black and white on its underside (see the picture on the opposite page). If they're turned on their backs the little frogs will keep perfectly still and 'play dead'.

The mossy home of the Corroboree frog

Corroboree frogs live only in swampy places high in the mountain ranges of south-eastern Australia.

The underside of a Corroboree frog

If you visit the Snowy Mountains in summer, you might hear the curious creaking call of the male frog. You're unlikely to see it, though. The frogs stay well hidden in their boggy homes, often living together in pairs. If the sphagnum bogs were destroyed, this little jewel of the mountains could easily become extinct.

Corroboree frogs differ from most other frogs because they lay just a few large eggs out of the water, not *in* the water. Their tadpoles develop almost entirely inside the egg. The tadpoles escape when rising water covers them after rain. (There's more about egg-laying on pages 23–4.)

The mating game

Most male and female frogs live separate lives and come together only to mate.

The female tree frog in the picture on the opposite page was attracted by the call of the smaller male. He is clasping her from behind with special pads on his hands. She will carry him to the water and they'll swim out to a suitable egg-laying site.

Two Great barred frogs on their way to the water to mate

The two Great barred frogs in the picture above are on their way to the nearest creek to start a new family. Once in the water the male, still clasping the female tightly, will pour fertilising fluid over her egg-mass, or spawn, as it comes out.

When a male frog clasps a female like this they are *in amplexus*, which simply means embracing. It is part of the special way frogs mate and fertilise their eggs.

The Great barred frog lives in wet forests where the leaf litter is cool and damp and easy to burrow under.

◄ *Peron's tree frogs before mating*

The male Brown-striped frog calls from the water's edge or among water plants to attract the female frog.

The frothy stuff is made of a substance like eggwhite and comes out with the eggs. The female beats it with her hands to embed the eggs in it. Only a few frogs lay their eggs in this way.

Brown-striped frogs mating

Spawn (frogs' eggs) in a pond

The second picture shows the mass of eggs, or spawn, as black specks among the bubbles. The jelly-like froth forms a floating raft which surrounds the eggs and protects them.

From below the water level you can see the newly hatched tadpoles still clinging to their raft.

The tadpole in the other picture has grown a pair of hind legs, and is on the way to being a frog.

Tadpoles hanging onto their frothy nest

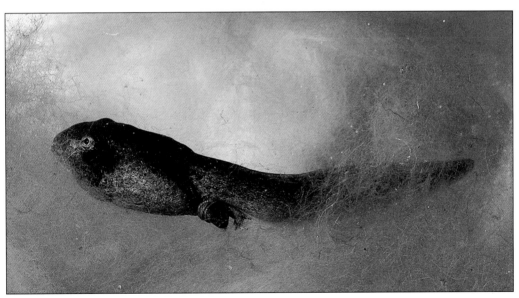

A Tadpole growing legs

The frogs we've looked at so far live around coastal and mountain areas where there is plenty of moisture. Let's look at some frogs that have found a way of surviving in the driest parts of Australia.

Tadpoles in an outback puddle

Going, going, gone to earth

Trilling frog soaking up water

The drought has broken and produced muddy puddles in an outback claypan. Frogs in the outback breed only when it rains, and lay their eggs in these temporary pools. The tadpoles develop quickly but evaporating rain puddles can sometimes leave them high and dry. Then they become easy victims for predators. The birds' footprints in the picture tell a grim story.

The water-holding frog in the small picture seems to be smiling as it soaks up the water through its skin. If it's a male frog he'll soon be calling for a female to share the puddle. If it's a female frog she'll be tuning into the local frog broadcast.

Trilling frog burying itself in the mud

Unlike their tadpoles, frogs in the outback can take steps to save themselves.

This one is about to go underground. How? Well, rainwater has evaporated, and left soft mud behind. Before the mud hardens during the next dry period, the frog will have safely buried itself.

Are you wondering about that white line across its eyes?

When humans go underwater, they put on goggles to protect their eyes. A frog's goggles are built in. When it dives or goes underground a transparent skin comes up from its lower eyelids like a shutter. The white line is the upper edge of the shutter.

Water-holding frog in its 'cocoon' of skin

Outback burrowing frogs store water in their kidneys to help them survive droughts.

We know that some animals in cold climates go into *hibernation*, which means 'winter sleep'. Desert frogs avoid drought by *aestivation* or 'summer sleep'.

The water-holding frog in the picture has made a small underground chamber. A 'cocoon' of transparent skin covers its whole body except its nostrils, sealing in moisture like a plastic wrapper.

Water-holding frogs have been known to survive up to nine years of drought, neither eating nor drinking nor moving in their cocoons.

Water-holding frog peeling off its protective skin

The water-holding frog becomes active again when rainwater comes seeping into the dry soil. Now it must get rid of the 'plastic wrapping' that kept it from drying out. It does this with its hands and feet, tearing at the skin, pulling it bit by bit over its head...and eating it!

Aboriginal people who lived in the desert used to dig up water-holding frogs and squeeze the water out of them! Not pleasant for the frogs, but a life-saver for a thirsty family.

'Watch-frogs' and frog-watchers

Green and golden bell frogs

Millions of years before there were people, frogs were filling the night with sound. Our earliest ancestors probably enjoyed the music of the frogs around their camp fires and in their caves at night as we do today.

Frogs will stop calling if there is any disturbance. Their continued chorus could have reassured our ancestors that there were no sabre-toothed tigers or great bears prowling in the night!

Can we still rely on frogs to warn us of danger? I for one still feel that primitive sense of safety at night as I listen to the 'watch-frogs' outside my bedroom window.

A small garden frog pond

Do you have a frog pond in your garden? Anything big enough to hold permanent water and a clump of water-loving plants can be a frog pond.

Water attracts birds and lizards and dragonflies as well as frogs. Best of all, a water garden is easy to look after—you don't have to water it! But remember, different kinds of frogs like different habitats. Catching frogs from somewhere else and putting them in your pond doesn't always work. Just supply the right kind of habitat and the frogs will appear from nowhere, all by themselves.

Frogs are fascinating and often beautiful little animals. But they are disappearing all around the world and no-one knows why.

You can help find out what's happening to Australian frogs by keeping a diary about the frogs in your garden. If you have a tape-recorder you could record their calls and make notes about where and when you heard them.

Or you can simply enjoy having the frogs around your home. Whatever you do—happy frog-watching!